WAKE LAZY BONES!

Written by Rochelle Larkin

Illustrated by Joe Dorety

Copyright © MCMXCII Playmore Inc., Publishers
and Waldman Publishing Corp., New York, New York
All rights reserved
Printed in China

Little Jackie didn't want to get out of bed. He liked to snuggle under the soft covers and dream about all the things he would do when he was big and strong.

He didn't want to think about what he should be doing now, like helping his mother, even though Little Jackie loved his mother and knew she had so much to do.

"Wake up, Lazybones!" his mother sang out,
"Breakfast is almost ready!"

Little Jackie knew that having his warm,
delicious breakfast would help him get big and strong.
But today he just wanted to stay under the covers.

Sometimes he just stayed in bed until his mother came and teased and tickled him until he got up. But today, Little Jackie decided, he was going to stay in bed ALL DAY.

"Hey, Lazybones, wake up!" a familiar voice called out. It was his friend, Davey the Duck.

"Guess where I've been!" Davey said. "I swam all the way down the creek to the big old oak tree on the bank. It took me over a hundred strokes!"

Little Jackie sat all the way up. "Wow!" he said, "that must have been hard."

Davey Duck looked very proud.

"My mother says I'm getting very strong. And I'm already the biggest duckling on the farm."

Davey looked at Little Jackie. "Do you want to come for a swim with me?" he asked.

"Not today, Davey," Little Jackie said.

"Well, goodbye then," said Davey, "I'm going out to have some more fun!"

Little Jackie's mother came to the door with a big bowl of cereal. Little Jackie could smell all the raisins and cinnamon and fruit.

"Now, Lazybones," said his mother, "you can't have any of this good breakfast til you come to the table to eat it." And she went back to the kitchen.

Little Jackie knew he should go into the woods for sticks and straws for the kitchen fire. But not today.

Little Jackie's mother was worried. Each time she peeped into Little Jackie's room, he was deeper and deeper under the covers.

"Wake up, Lazybones!" a voice called in from the window. It was Robin, who lived in the big apple tree outside.

"I just brought the biggest twig I ever carried for our new nest," Robin chirped. "Come and help me find another big twig!" He fluttered his wings up and down and gripped the window sill with his shiny claws.

"Not today," said Little Jackie. "I'm just going to stay in bed all day."

"What kind of fun is that?" chirped Robin, as he spread his wings and flew a loop-de-loop into the room and out again through the window.

"I'm out of here!"

Now to get some real rest, Little Jackie thought. His friends were all gone to the forest. But then he heard a familiar buzzing sound.

"Bzzz, bzzz, Lazybzzones!" hummed Buzzy Bee, as his shiny yellow and black body came swooping all over Little Jackie's room. "This is no time to be in bed! It's time to find some honey!"

Little Jackie was hungry, and thought it would be nice to taste some of Buzzy's sweet honey. But it was too much work.

"Not today, Buzzy," said Little Jackie. He pulled the covers back up to his chin.

"Bzz-bye, bzz-bye, then," said Buzzy Bee as he flew out into the sunshine. "I'll find my sunny honey by myself."

Little Jackie tried to get back to sleep.
It was hard work doing nothing. It made him tired.

He snuggled under the covers again.
This time, he pulled them right over his head!

It was dark under the covers, like the inside of a deep cave. Suddenly, Little Jackie saw a big shape coming towards him.

It was a giant grizzly bear, shaking his head and rubbing his eyes.

"What a long time I've slept," he growled. "What I need now is a good meal!"

Little Jackie kept very still. He didn't want to be the first thing that big bear saw when he woke up, angry and hungry.

No sooner had the bear gone looking for food than another shape stretched itself out in the darkness. A tiger, crouching low, sprang up.

"It looks like night time," growled the tiger, "time for me to be hunting my next meal."

Little Jackie tried to make himself even smaller. He wanted to stay out of the way of that tiger! But as the tiger slunk away, Little Jackie heard a mighty roar.

There was a lion, shaking his giant mane, crowding Little Jackie to the furthest corner of his bed.

"I want my dinner now!' the lion roared.

Little Jackie jumped out of bed. He ran to the kitchen and hugged his mother tightly.

"Scary things happen when you stay in bed too long," he said. "I want my breakfast now. Then I'm going to get all the sticks and straw you need from the forest." His mother gave him a big kiss.

"I'm going to eat my breakfast and get big," said Little Jackie. "I'm going to do my chores and get strong. I'm not going to be 'Lazybones' any more!"

All of Little Jackie's friends were waiting outside to go with him.

And he never wanted to spend all day in bed again!